Samuel French Acting Edition

The River Bride

by Marisela Treviño Orta

D1602332

ı|SAMUEL FRENCH|ı

Copyright © 2020 by Marisela Treviño Orta
All Rights Reserved

THE RIVER BRIDE is fully protected under the copyright laws of the United States of America, the British Commonwealth, including Canada, and all member countries of the Berne Convention for the Protection of Literary and Artistic Works, the Universal Copyright Convention, and/ or the World Trade Organization conforming to the Agreement on Trade Related Aspects of Intellectual Property Rights. All rights, including professional and amateur stage productions, recitation, lecturing, public reading, motion picture, radio broadcasting, television and the rights of translation into foreign languages are strictly reserved.

ISBN 978-0-573-70896-1

www.concordtheatricals.com
www.concordtheatricals.co.uk

FOR PRODUCTION ENQUIRIES

UNITED STATES AND CANADA
info@concordtheatricals.com
1-866-979-0447

UNITED KINGDOM AND EUROPE
licensing@concordtheatricals.co.uk
020-7054-7200

Each title is subject to availability from Concord Theatricals Corp., depending upon country of performance. Please be aware that *THE RIVER BRIDE* may not be licensed by Concord Theatricals Corp. in your territory. Professional and amateur producers should contact the nearest Concord Theatricals Corp. office or licensing partner to verify availability.

CAUTION: Professional and amateur producers are hereby warned that *THE RIVER BRIDE* is subject to a licensing fee. The purchase, renting, lending or use of this book does not constitute a license to perform this title(s), which license must be obtained from Concord Theatricals Corp. prior to any performance. Performance of this title(s) without a license is a violation of federal law and may subject the producer and/or presenter or such performances to civil penalties. A licensing fee must be paid whether the title(s) is presented for charity or gain and whether or not admission is charged. Professional/Stock licensing fees are quoted upon application to Concord Theatricals Corp.

This work is published by Samuel French, an imprint of Concord Theatricals Corp.

No one shall make any changes in this title(s) for the purpose of production. No part of this book may be reproduced, stored in a retrieval system, or transmitted in any form, by any means, now known or yet to be invented, including mechanical, electronic, photocopying, recording, videotaping, or otherwise, without the prior written permission of the publisher. No one shall upload this title(s), or part of this title(s), to any social media websites.

For all enquiries regarding motion picture, television, and other media rights, please contact Concord Theatricals Corp.

MUSIC USE NOTE

Licensees are solely responsible for obtaining formal written permission from copyright owners to use copyrighted music in the performance of this play and are strongly cautioned to do so. If no such permission is obtained by the licensee, then the licensee must use only original music that the licensee owns and controls. Licensees are solely responsible and liable for all music clearances and shall indemnify the copyright owners of the play(s) and their licensing agent, Concord Theatricals Corp., against any costs, expenses, losses and liabilities arising from the use of music by licensees. Please contact the appropriate music licensing authority in your territory for the rights to any incidental music.

IMPORTANT BILLING AND CREDIT REQUIREMENTS

If you have obtained performance rights to this title, please refer to your licensing agreement for important billing and credit requirements.

THE RIVER BRIDE was first produced by the Oregon Shakespeare Festival (Bill Rauch, Artistic Director; Cynthia Rider, Executive Director) in Ashland, Oregon on February 21, 2016. The performance was directed by Laurie Woolery, with sets by Mariana Sánchez, costumes by Raquel Barreto, lights by David Weiner, composition and sound by Bruno Louchouarn, video by Mark Holthusen, movement by Sarah Lozoff, dramaturgy by Nakissa Etemad, voice and speech direction by Robert Ramirez, and fight direction by Christopher DuVal. The production stage manager was Moira Gleason. The cast was as follows:

HELENA / ENSEMBLE . . . . Nancy Rodriguez

BELMIRA / ENSEMBLE . . . . Jamie Ann Romero

MOISES / ENSEMBLE . . . . Armando McClain

DUARTE / ENSEMBLE . . . . Carlo Albán

SR. COSTA / ENSEMBLE . . . . Triney Sandoval

SRA. COSTA / ENSEMBLE . . . . Vilma Silva

THE RIVER BRIDE was developed in residency with AlterTheater Ensemble in San Rafael, California.

CHARACTERS

HELENA – (18) Smart and a beauty in her own right, though not as outgoing as her sister Belmira.

BELMIRA – (16) Beautiful, frivolous and a bit vain, but charming and adored by the entire village. She is the bride to be and has an appetite for adventure.

MOISES – (20-25) Charming, handsome, and mysterious. Earnest and sympathetic, he's been searching for love for a long time. Wears a bandage over his forehead, which he never removes. Dressed like a man of property.

DUARTE – (20-25) A good man from a respected family. He is the groom to be.

SR. COSTA – (Late 40s) Belmira and Helena's father. A fisherman.

SRA. COSTA – (Late 40s) Belmira and Helena's mother.

SETTING

In a small Brazilian village along the Amazon River.

TIME

Once upon a time.

AUTHOR'S NOTES

NOTE ON CHARACTER

Belmira is a complicated character. Do not reduce her to a villain. Blaming her for the failure of Helena and Duarte's relationship or Helena and Moises's relationship should be avoided. Those relationships failed because the people in them failed one another. The complexity and nuance of these failed relationships will help prevent Belmira from being seen as a villain. Finally, the point of the play is that Helena and Moises fail one another out of fear – fear of the unknown, fear of being alone.

NOTE ON CASTING

Ages of characters should not be strictly adhered to when casting roles. Feel free to cast older actors who embody the sense of youth needed for each role.

PORTUGUESE WORDS AND PHRASES

a mão, filho: a hand, son (asking for assistance)

a minha e eu: me and mine (as in my wife)

a minha mulher: my woman

amor: love, darling

amor meu: my love

ao seu serviço: at your service

boa tarde: good afternoon

boto: dolphin

chega: that's enough

claro que sim: yes/of course (emphatic)

comadres: close friends

é um milagre: it's a miracle

encantado: delighted (as in, "delighted to meet you")

então me diga: then tell me

filha: daughter

gatinho lindo: handsome man/handsome one

irmã: sister

irmãzinha: little sister

mãe: mother/mom

menininha: little girl

muito bem: well done

nada: nothing

nossa senhora: our lady (referring to the Virgin Mary)

olha: consider or note an idea

onde você está?: where are you?

pai: father

pirarucu: one of the largest freshwater fish in the world

qual é o problema: what's the matter?/what's wrong?

quem sabe: who knows

querida/o: dear/darling

senhor: mister

te acalma: calm down

PRELUDE TO *THE RIVER BRIDE*
for Kathy Roberts

In the Amazon time stands still, as if this river wrapped its long body around it and contracted. The only time here is once, once upon a time somewhere between dream, between myth, between the shores of reality, and folklore.

Like all the old ones this fairy tale will end in tears, tears spilling off the edge of a pier. It will end with two sisters, one constrained to land and one to the Amazon's timeless embrace. Two sisters, two sisters, and a man fished from June waters just three days before a wedding.

Scene One

(In the dark the sound of splashing, as if something small is being thrown into a body of water, followed by dolphin clicks of approval. Spotlight comes up slowly on the end of a long pier that runs the width of the stage. Late afternoon. Stage right the pier stops short a bit, where it is surrounded by the Amazon River. Sitting at the end of the pier is BELMIRA, barefoot and beautiful. Her legs swinging over the end of the dock, intermittently she tosses small fish into the river. The sound of something swimming and splashing is heard.)

(One splash almost gets BELMIRA wet. She laughs.)

BELMIRA. *(To dolphin.)* You don't look so lonely to me.

That's what they say around here: That *botos* are cursed with loneliness. Cursed to swim these dark waters, searching for a way out.

I know exactly how that feels.

Just how did your kind get stuck in this river so far inland?

I wonder...have you forgotten the taste of seawater? And the muddy Amazon has made you almost blind. Tell me, *boto*, do you ever dream of the ocean, of water so clear and blue you can see for miles?

(Pause.)

I'm getting married, *boto*. In three days I'll be Duarte's wife. And he'll work hard and save up enough money to take us downstream. We'll move to a real city. No more village. No more river. Instead we'll have an ocean view. I'm going to see the world, *boto*.

He's going to do it. It's his wedding gift to me. I asked him to promise to take me to the coast. And the best thing about Duarte – aside from being the most handsome man in the village – is that he's a man of his word.

> *(Enter* **HELENA** *from stage left, a basket on her hip. She wears a corsage orchid, Cattleya labiata, in her hair.)*

HELENA. Belmira.

> *(***BELMIRA** *ignores her.)*

Belmira, I've been looking for you.

BELMIRA. I've been here.

HELENA. Hiding from your chores?

BELMIRA. Why should I do chores? In three days I'll be a married woman living in my very own home.

HELENA. Your very own home will still need cleaning.

BELMIRA. I'll ask Duarte to hire a maid.

HELENA. A maid?! And who in the village do you plan to hire? All the women already have enough work keeping their own homes.

BELMIRA. When we move to the city we can get a maid. Everyone has a maid there.

> *(***BELMIRA** *tosses in another fish. More splashing from somewhere out of sight.)*

HELENA. What are you doing?

BELMIRA. Making friends.

HELENA. If our father catches you wasting his bait, he'll tan your hide. Wedding or not.

BELMIRA. What's a few fish? *Pai* gives away fish all the time.

HELENA. To <u>people</u>.

> *(From the water comes the sound of disapproving clicks.)*

BELMIRA. Look, you offended him.

HELENA. Pouting won't work on me, Belmira. I know all your tricks.

BELMIRA. *(Laughs.)* All part of a woman's arsenal. Something we all must master.

HELENA. Some more than others.

BELMIRA. *(Darker.)* ...Yes. Some more than others.

> (**BELMIRA** *throws in another fish.*)

HELENA. If you keep feeding that dolphin, it'll come back.

BELMIRA. That's the idea. He can be the guest of honor at my wedding.

HELENA. Those things are all mischief.

BELMIRA. That's just an old wives' tale.

HELENA. It'll mess with *pai*'s nets. Steal his fish.

BELMIRA. I think they're good luck. The more I feed him, the more money Duarte will make.

HELENA. Money can't buy happiness, *irmãzinha*.

BELMIRA. You ever notice how it's people without money who tend to say that?
(To dolphin.) Here's one last fish, *gatinho lindo*. This one is to make sure Duarte keeps his promise and takes me to the city.

> (*The sound of splashing.*)

Wait! Where are you going?

> (*Thunder. A fierce lightning storm approaches.*)

HELENA. Come inside, Belmira. It's going to rain.

BELMIRA. It's always going to rain.

> (*A bolt of colored lightning illuminates the sky pink.*)

Wait, did you see that?

HELENA. It's just lightning.

BELMIRA. But I've never seen lightning like that before. Maybe it's for me. The heavens are putting on a show, announcing my wedding with a drum roll all of Brazil can hear.

HELENA. It's just a storm.

BELMIRA. No, don't you feel it? There's something in the air. A charge.

> *(It begins to rain.* **BELMIRA**, *childlike, relishes getting wet.* **BELMIRA** *extends her hand to her sister, a peace offering. Initially* **HELENA** *covers her head, but watching her sister's reverie,* **HELENA** *uncovers her head and enjoys the rain.)*

> *(A flash of lightning and the side of the stage where the sisters stand goes dark. Coinciding with the lights down stage right a spotlight quickly comes up stage left on* **SR. COSTA** *and* **DUARTE**. *They are set apart from the rest of the staging, in a boat on the river.)*

SR. COSTA. Did you see that?

DUARTE. What?

SR. COSTA. The lightning. It was…

DUARTE. It was what?

SR. COSTA. *(Searching.)* Something familiar…something I used to know.

> *(He shakes it off.)*

The nets. We need to pull the nets in now.

> *(The men begin to pull in the nets.)*

DUARTE. Umph! Feel that? Even in a downpour you fill your nets.

SR. COSTA. The weight. It doesn't feel as it should.

DUARTE. We'll have plenty for the banquet now.

SR. COSTA. Duarte.
It's not fish.

> *(Suddenly, from the net, a man's arm comes up over the side of the boat. The rest of the*

*man is hidden from view by the boat. His
arm, which is well dressed in a white cotton
suit, is limp yet not lifeless.)*

(Astonished.) Nossa senhora.

(Urgent.) Into the boat. Get him into the boat.

*(Lightning flashes again and lights on the
men quickly come down. Lights back up on
HELENA and **BELMIRA**. They stand in the rain
laughing.)*

HELENA. Come on!

*(They head stage left. Lights up on the rest of
the stage revealing the small one-room home
of the Costa family, its interior visible. The
sisters go inside their home. **BELMIRA** shakes
herself dry, **HELENA** laughs.)*

*(Lightning strikes much closer and thunder
shakes everything.)*

*(As the thunder dissipates, offstage voices are
heard.)*

SR. COSTA. *(Offstage.)* Move. Move.

*(**SR. COSTA** and **DUARTE** enter carrying
MOISES. They are followed by **SRA. COSTA**
who holds the gentleman's hat. **MOISES** is
unconscious, his head bandaged. He wears a
white cotton suit and wears black dress shoes.
SR. COSTA and **DUARTE** bring **MOISES** into the
house and put him on the bed.)*

HELENA. What's going on?

BELMIRA. Who is that?

SRA. COSTA. No one knows. Your father pulled him out of
the river.

SR. COSTA. We were bringing in the nets, because of the
storm and I felt something on the other end. Thought
maybe a *pirarucu* had gotten tangled in our net. But
what do I find? Not a fish, but a man.

(To **DUARTE**.*)* Careful with his head.

HELENA. What happened to him?

SR. COSTA. *Quem sabe.* It was already bandaged like that.

BELMIRA. Where do you think he's from?

DUARTE. Dressed like that? Not from around here.

BELMIRA. You're right. Look at his shoes. Not a scuff. They're completely brand new.

SRA. COSTA. All his clothes are.

HELENA. What could he be doing here?

BELMIRA. Fishing?

DUARTE. He's no fisherman.

SR. COSTA. What then?

DUARTE. We'll have to ask him when he wakes.

> (**HELENA** *picks up* **MOISES**'s *hat.*)

HELENA. Is this his?

DUARTE. I think so.

The light's almost gone.

(To **SR. COSTA**.*)* We should go back to the river. If he was traveling with others –

SR. COSTA. Yes, yes. Good idea. Come, Duarte.

> (**SR. COSTA** *begins to leave.* **DUARTE** *stops him.*)

DUARTE. Shouldn't one of us stay?

SR. COSTA. If there's someone else out there I'll need your help to get them out of the river.

BELMIRA. It's all right, Duarte. The three of us can manage.

> (**DUARTE** *acquiesces with a nod.*)

SR. COSTA. All right then. We'll be back soon.

> (**SR. COSTA** *and* **DUARTE** *exit.*)

> (**SRA. COSTA** *brings a bowl of water and a small cloth to* **HELENA**.*)

SRA. COSTA. Helena, here, why don't you tend to our guest. We'll make him something to eat.

BELMIRA. Why does Helena get to nurse him?

SRA. COSTA. Because Helena isn't engaged to be married.

HELENA. *(Slightly vexed.)* Mãe.

SRA. COSTA. What? There's no harm in it. And by the looks of it, he comes from a good family.

HELENA. You mean "wealthy," *Mãe.* And clothes do not make a man good.

BELMIRA. But they can make him more pleasing to look at.

HELENA. *(Admonishing.)* Belmira.

BELMIRA. What? I'm not married yet.

> *(***BELMIRA*** *takes the cloth and bowl from* **HELENA***.)*

Besides, I'm a much better nurse than you are.

> *(***BELMIRA*** *sits on the bed and begins to clean* **MOISES***'s face.* **HELENA** *and* **SRA. COSTA** *prepare something for* **MOISES** *to eat.)*

He's very handsome.

HELENA. No more handsome than Duarte.

BELMIRA. I wonder how he hurt his head.

> *(***BELMIRA*** *inspects the bandage.)*

HELENA. Leave it alone, Belmira. He's wearing it for a reason.

> *(After a moment,* **BELMIRA** *tries to lift the bandage to look underneath it. As she touches the bandage* **MOISES** *awakens and stops her. Meanwhile the rainstorm tapers off, coinciding with* **MOISES** *awakening.)*

BELMIRA. I'm sorry. I thought maybe you'd want a new dressing.

MOISES. Thank you, but this one will do.

> *(***MOISES*** *attempts to sit up a bit.)*

BELMIRA. Careful. You need to rest.

MOISES. Where am I?

BELMIRA. Safe. This is my parents' home. My father pulled you out of the river.

MOISES. Out of its embrace...and into another.

Tell me, what is your name?

BELMIRA. Belmira.

MOISES. Bel-mira. "Beautiful to look upon." You most certainly are.

I am Moises.

> (**MOISES** *takes* **BELMIRA***'s hand and kisses it, which pleases her.*)

> (**SRA. COSTA** *and* **HELENA** *approach with food.*)

SRA. COSTA. Sir, you are welcome in our home.

MOISES. Thank you. You are very kind.

SRA. COSTA. These are my daughters Belmira and Helena.

> (**MOISES** *and* **HELENA** *are caught in a glance.* **SRA. COSTA** *and* **BELMIRA** *notice.*)

MOISES. *(To* **HELENA***.) Encantado.*

(To all.) Moises Lira, *ao seu serviço.*

SRA. COSTA. My husband is looking for someone who might know you. Were you traveling with anyone?

MOISES. No, I was alone. I always travel alone.

HELENA. Where were you going?

MOISES. Every year I make this trip up river.

BELMIRA. Every year. You must have your own boat.

SRA. COSTA. Your boat! It must have gone down in the storm.

HELENA. Do you remember what happened?

MOISES. I was trying to come ashore... I must have lost my balance. I don't remember much more.

HELENA. And your head?

MOISES. This? The day before last I ran into a tree.

BELMIRA. *(Incredulous.)* Ran into a tree?

MOISES. Sometimes I have trouble...my eyesight. I made a quick turn and hit my head. It's fine though.

HELENA. It doesn't hurt?

MOISES. No. Not at all.

SRA. COSTA. You're very fortunate. It's a miracle you didn't drown.

MOISES. Well, I'm very much at home in the water. I can almost swim in my sleep.

BELMIRA. And your boat? Was it very big?

HELENA. *(Admonishing.)* Belmira.

BELMIRA. What? I'm just trying to make conversation.

MOISES. No. Not very big at all. I prefer something simple. A raft is much easier to pull ashore when all you have is yourself.

HELENA. That's very practical.

MOISES. I try to be. Whenever I have the chance.

BELMIRA. Well, everyone's very practical here. That's why we all live in this one room.

MOISES. *(To* **SRA. COSTA.***)* I think you have a very charming home.

SRA. COSTA. Thank you.

*(***SR. COSTA** *and* **DUARTE** *return.)*

SR. COSTA. Nothing. We didn't find anyone or anything.

SRA. COSTA. *Amor,* this is Moises Lira. He says he was traveling alone.

(To **MOISES.***)* This is my husband and Duarte. He and Belmira are marrying in just a few days.

MOISES. Sir, I am in your debt.

*(***MOISES** *attempts to rise but is weak.)*

SR. COSTA. Rest. Rest. Let's hear no more talk about "debt." We've fished you out of the river, so you're our responsibility. You are most welcome to stay here with us for as long as you need.

SRA. COSTA. Yes, please. You must stay for Belmira's wedding. You would be a guest of honor at the ceremony.

MOISES. Then I dare not refuse. Thank you. Thank you for taking me into your home.

> (**MOISES** *looks at* **HELENA**. *Everyone notices. Lights shift.*)

Scene Two

(Sunrise comes up and brightens into a new day.)

(Midday. Lights up on **BELMIRA** *in a very simple white dress. She stands on a small crate while* **SRA. COSTA** *removes pins on the newly sewn hem of the dress. Kneeling,* **HELENA** *takes the pins from her mother.)*

(Two days until the wedding.)

BELMIRA. He's probably traveled all over the world. I wonder... I wonder how rich he is.

HELENA. Who?

BELMIRA. You know exactly who I'm talking about, Helena. In fact, it's the only person anyone in this village can talk about. So don't pretend you aren't thinking about him, too. We all are.

HELENA. What does it matter how rich he is?

BELMIRA. Why? Because I already have a husband? There are still two days 'til my wedding, so there's no harm in me speculating about another man.

HELENA. Are you trying to convince me, or yourself?

SRA. COSTA. Girls, please.

HELENA. ...And that's not what I meant.

BELMIRA. No?

HELENA. No. I meant to say a man's worth isn't in the money he holds.

SRA. COSTA. Very true, *filha*. Very true.

BELMIRA. *Então me diga.* What do you make of him?

HELENA. ...I can't say yet.

BELMIRA. Come on, Helena. Tell me what you thought at first glance – and that was some glance, *irmã* – what did you make of him?

HELENA. ...I...I was bewildered.

(**SRA. COSTA** *responds to this.*)

    I felt a little frightened.

BELMIRA. Frightened? Of him?

HELENA. No...of myself.

    I couldn't help thinking...

BELMIRA. What?

HELENA. That he's like something shiny you see in the water. And when you reach in to grab it, you end up losing your hand.

    (**BELMIRA** *laughs.*)

BELMIRA. Oh, Helena. That is why Love is for the bold. You have to be willing to risk everything to get what you want.

HELENA. At all costs?

BELMIRA. *Que sim.* In the end, the only tally that matters is how many regrets you have.

SRA. COSTA. *Chega*, enough. Both of you. If only you two were as wise as you sound.

    There is more yet for the world to teach you. Live another sixteen years, Belmira before you talk about living with regret.

    Words are good for a lot of things, but Love lives in a place deep inside you where there are no words. No words. That's why it's so hard to understand.

    (*To* **HELENA.**) But, *filha*, you will know it. You will recognize it. I have faith that you will.

    (**MOISES** *enters and knocks on the frame of the home's door.*)

MOISES. May I?

BELMIRA. It's bad luck for you to see me in my wedding dress.

HELENA. Bad luck for the groom, Belmira.

    (**MOISES** *approaches* **HELENA.** *From behind his back he reveals a parcel.*)

MOISES. *(To* HELENA.*)* I've brought you something.

> (HELENA, *unsure, does not take the parcel.*
> BELMIRA *steps in and takes it.)*

BELMIRA. *(Excited.)* What is it?

MOISES. I thought your sister might like a new dress of her own.

BELMIRA. Well, let's see.

> (BELMIRA *opens the parcel. Inside is the most*
> *exquisite ivory silk. She holds it up, letting it*
> *cascade down.)*

Oh! It's beautiful. *Mãe*, look. So soft and cool. *Mãe*, feel it. Like water running through your fingers.

SRA. COSTA. *Senhor* Lira, you are too kind.

BELMIRA. It's perfect. Perfect!

Mãe, we have to sew another wedding dress.

SRA. COSTA. Belmira, please. This was meant for Helena.

BELMIRA. ...Oh, of course. *Senhor* Lira, you must forgive me. I just thought. I mean, it's such fine material. So much nicer than my own.

And Helena wouldn't mind. Would you, *irmã*? I mean, not for your own sister's wedding dress?

HELENA. ...But... Belmira. Do you think there's enough time to sew a new dress? Your wedding is in two days.

BELMIRA. That's plenty of time. Especially if we have help.

Mãe, all we have to do is ask your c*omadres*.

SRA. COSTA. ...Helena?

HELENA. She's right, *Mãe*. The dress you make from that silk is the kind a woman only wears once in her life.

Senhor Lira?

MOISES. Helena, it is yours to do with as you will.

> (HELENA *nods in capitulation.* BELMIRA *hugs*
> *her.)*

BELMIRA. Oh thank you, Helena! Thank you!

Mãe, come on, you'll have to get your *comadres* to start right away.

SRA. COSTA. Well, you'll have to be the one doing the asking, *menininha.*

BELMIRA. And how could anyone say, "no" to a bride to be?

> *(**SRA. COSTA** grabs a change of clothes for **BELMIRA** from the bed and begins to herd her out the door.)*

SRA. COSTA. In the meantime, Helena, why don't you and *Senhor* Lira go for a walk?

BELMIRA. Why can't I walk with him? I should be the one thanking him.

SRA. COSTA. Because you've got to ask my *comadres* to sew you a new dress. Come on now.

> *(**BELMIRA** and **SRA. COSTA** exit. A moment before **HELENA** speaks.)*

HELENA. I don't know where to take you.

MOISES. How about the pier? I always enjoy being near the water.

HELENA. Even after what happened?

MOISES. What happened?

HELENA. You almost drowned.

MOISES. But I didn't.

> *(**MOISES** moves aside to allow **HELENA** to exit the house. They walk along to the end of the pier.)*

That was very gracious, what you sacrificed for your sister back there.

HELENA. It's something I've grown accustomed to. Besides, there are some things that aren't worth fighting over.

MOISES. And others that are?

HELENA. Of course. I prefer to choose my battles for what truly matters.

MOISES. Very wisely put. But you still deserve a dress of your own. I will have to get you some more of that silk.

HELENA. That would be quite a feat. I've never seen anything like it before here in our village.

MOISES. I have my ways.

HELENA. Even without a boat?

MOISES. I can be very persuasive.

HELENA. So you're not stranded here.

MOISES. ...No.

HELENA. Then why do you stay?

MOISES. Because I desire to.

(**MOISES** *approaches* **HELENA**.)

I have something else for you.

(*From behind* **HELENA***'s ear* **MOISES** *produces a necklace, the pendant a lone pearl. He holds it out for her. She doesn't take it. After a moment he laughs.*)

Your sister would have already had it around her neck by now.

HELENA. I am not my sister.

MOISES. No, you're more discerning.

HELENA. (*Slightly flustered.*) What do you mean?

MOISES. You can see past the surface of someone. See them for who they truly are. And when you give your love it will be genuine. The kind of love that can change a man, keep him firmly planted on the ground.

HELENA. ...I... You surprise me, sir.

MOISES. Please, Helena. Call me Moises.

HELENA. ...Moises.

(**HELENA** *reaches to take the necklace.* **MOISES** *closes his hand around hers, brings her hand up to his lips and kisses it.*)

I'm not used to men who flatter. It can feel... disingenuous.

MOISES. I know it can. But I mean it. Most sincerely.

Time forces me to be direct. I don't have the luxury of a more measured courtship, Helena. And courting is exactly what I intend to do with the short time I've been given.

You asked me what keeps me here. You are why I stay.

> (**HELENA** *moves away from him a bit, untrusting.*)

But if you don't trust my words, that's all right. For me there are no words.

HELENA. *(A realization.)* "No words."

MOISES. None. None that can penetrate deep inside me, that can travel the line inside me that goes to you. You can only recognize it. Like seeing your reflection in the water. It's something you feel. And then know.

HELENA. You are right. You are very direct…but I like it.

> (**HELENA** *begins to put the necklace on.*)

MOISES. Please, allow me.

> (**MOISES** *puts the necklace on* **HELENA**. **BELMIRA** *enters and watches from a distance.*)

> (*Once again* **MOISES** *and* **HELENA** *are caught in a glance. The couple searches one another's faces.)*

HELENA. …Like seeing your reflection in the water.

MOISES. It's something you feel.

HELENA. And then know.

> (*Just when it appears that* **MOISES** *and* **HELENA** *are about to kiss,* **BELMIRA** *interrupts.*)

BELMIRA. *Senhor* Lira, there you are.

MOISES. As you find me.

BELMIRA. You have to let me properly thank you for the material. Both Duarte and I are so grateful. He wants to tell you himself. Come.

> (**BELMIRA** *links her arm around* **MOISES**'s *and begins to walk him away from* **HELENA** *and off the pier to exit stage left.)*

Then I'm going to take you on a proper walk. Show you all our little village has to offer.

(**MOISES** *carefully liberates his arm from* **BELMIRA**.)

MOISES. I can hardly wait.

Helena...

(**MOISES** *offers* **HELENA** *his arm.* **HELENA** *accepts his arm and then with more confidence leads* **MOISES** *past* **BELMIRA** *and then offstage.* **BELMIRA** *follows, slightly disappointed. The sun sets as lights shift into night.*)

Scene Three

(The sounds of nighttime in the jungle decrescendo as light transitions to dawn. Sunrise and then midday light comes up. **SR. COSTA** *and* **DUARTE** *in a boat on the river approach the pier.* **DUARTE** *jumps out of the boat and ties their boat line to the pier. The men unpack their nets, ropes.)*

(One day until the wedding.)

DUARTE. Do you trust him?

SR. COSTA. Why shouldn't I?

DUARTE. No one knows anything about him. Where he's from. His family.

SR. COSTA. And if you knew these things, you'd feel better about him and Helena?

DUARTE. ...No, not really.

SR. COSTA. Duarte, what you are feeling, it's natural. You're practically family. You feel...overprotective. It's not easy to see someone you care about with someone else.

DUARTE. That's not it.
I don't trust him.

SR. COSTA. And do you trust Helena? Her judgment?

DUARTE. Of course.

SR. COSTA. As do I. Besides. I have a feeling about Moises. There's something familiar about him.

DUARTE. Familiar?

SR. COSTA. Yes. As if he's a kindred spirit. I sense goodness in him, Duarte. That's all.

DUARTE. Hmm.

(The men sit on the pier and soak their feet in the river.)

SR. COSTA. Ahhh...feel that?

DUARTE. *(Almost nervous.)* What?

SR. COSTA. Rainwater from Bolivia. Silt from Colombia. Oh, if this river could put its mouth to my ear – the secrets it would impart.

Forgive me. I'm just a sentimental old man. How time has passed, keeping pace with this river no less. I remember when my girls were taking their first trembling steps. And now my youngest daughter marries tomorrow evening.

May you two have as many years of happiness as *a minha e eu.*

DUARTE. Thank you, *Senhor* Costa.

SR. COSTA. Marriage has been very good to me, Duarte. Changed the entire course of my life.

DUARTE. Did it?

SR. COSTA. Oh, yes. That's its gift. With the right woman, Love could redirect the entire Amazon. Draw the ocean upstream.

A minha mulher did. Oh the power her heavenly body had over my rivers and tides. Has, I should say. Yes, marriage has been very good to me, as it will be to you, Duarte.

DUARTE. Thank you.

(**MOISES** *enters and approaches the men.*)

MOISES. *Boa tarde.* How was the day's catch?

SR. COSTA. Terrible. Our nets came back completely empty. That hasn't happened in...well...never. I've always had a way with this river, but I suppose there's a first time for everything. I'm only sorry we have nothing to bring to tonight's banquet.

MOISES. Perhaps I can help.

DUARTE. Do you know anything about fishing?

MOISES. A little.

DUARTE. "A little"? We aren't doing this for leisure. We're trying to feed our families.

SR. COSTA. Duarte, *te acalma.*

Senhor Lira, please be my guest.

(**SR. COSTA** *offers* **MOISES** *the net.* **MOISES**
gathers the net into his hands as if into a
small ball. In one graceful gesture he throws
it. The net expands and falls into the river.)

Muito bem! You <u>have</u> fished before.

MOISES. Yes, well, like you I've become very adept at
catching my dinner from this river.

DUARTE. I would have thought your servants would do that
for you.

MOISES. You would have thought wrong. I do not have
servants. Nor do I have need for any. Whatever I need
done, I can do myself.

SR. COSTA. You're a man's man, Moises. Sit. Join us.

(**MOISES** *sits, removes his shoes and socks and*
puts his feet into the river.)

MOISES. Hmmm...feel that?

DUARTE. What?

MOISES. The river. How it pulses with life. It's like
submerging into the heartbeat of a continent.

SR. COSTA. *(Excited.)* It speaks to you, too?

MOISES. All the time.

SR. COSTA. Ah...that's how it was when I was younger. We
have a lot in common, Moises. Before I met my wife,
I... I...

MOISES. What is it?

SR. COSTA. It's funny. I almost don't remember my life
before. As if it were a dream, a haze I wandered
through. And when I saw her that first time, it was like
coming out from under a spell. Like seeing the world
clearly.

I can still see her. Standing on the pier.

That day, that first day, I can always picture it so
distinctly. But it's as if she erased everything that came
before it.

MOISES. You don't remember anything from before that
day?

SR. COSTA. The old memories, they surface every now and then – when I try to grab onto them they slip through my fingers like smoke.

Don't listen to me. I must be getting old. My mind must be starting to go.

DUARTE. Nonsense. You're the best fisherman in the village.

SR. COSTA. Speaking of fish, perhaps it's time we bring in your haul.

> (DUARTE and MOISES begin to pull the net back in.)

DUARTE. The net's caught on something. You snagged it.

MOISES. I don't think so.

> (The net continues to come in, but it's obviously very heavy. It takes all three of them to haul the very full net onto the pier and brings them to their knees. The sound of fish writhing, flopping.)

SR. COSTA. *Nossa senhora, é um milagre!* Look! Enough fish for tonight's banquet and then some. Duarte, can you believe it?

DUARTE. *(Confounded.)* ...Beginner's luck.

SR. COSTA. Beginner or not, however long you were planning to stay in our village, I entreat you: stay longer. We could use this kind of luck as long as you can spare it, Moises.

> (SR. COSTA begins to get up off his knees. He reaches out for assistance.)

A mão, filho.

> (Both DUARTE and MOISES offer their arm to help SR. COSTA get up. SR. COSTA accepts MOISES's arm, and in this moment of connection the two men seem to grow closer. DUARTE is clearly disappointed.)

Thank you.

DUARTE. Excuse me.

*(DUARTE leaves. MOISES and SR. COSTA watch
him exit.)*

MOISES. I'm afraid I've disturbed the waters here.

SR. COSTA. Duarte is a good man. He doesn't give his trust
easily. But don't worry, he'll come around. At least
enough to respect you.

MOISES. It's not his respect I hope to earn, *Senhor* Costa.
It's yours.

SR. COSTA. That reminds me. I want to thank you for the
material you gave my daughter. Belmira is overjoyed.
She won't stop talking about it.

MOISES. You're most welcome.

SR. COSTA. But you should work on your aim.

MOISES. Sir?

SR. COSTA. Next time you have something to give Helena,
make sure it stays with her.

MOISES. Yes. Well, I already have.

SR. COSTA. Really? Good for you. And as for gaining my
respect, that's easy enough, Moises. Treat my daughter
well. Love her truly. Honestly.

MOISES. I intend to.

SR. COSTA. Good. Good.
Come. We should get this fish cleaned.

(The men sit and clean fish.)

(Beat.)

MOISES. I don't mean to intrude. Do you mind if I ask you
something?

SR. COSTA. Go right ahead.

MOISES. Where I come from we tell stories. They travel like
echoes and reverberate through our whole lives. Stories
about becoming a man. About the ones who didn't
settle, who searched until they found it. True love.
Stories about men...like you.

SR. COSTA. Like me?

MOISES. Yes. In fact, exactly like you.

Would you believe I grew up hearing your story over and over again?

SR. COSTA. But I'm just a simple fisherman.

MOISES. No, *compadre*. You're much more than that.

You said you couldn't really remember your life before meeting your wife. Could you try? For me?

I know I have no right to ask, but I need to know how you managed to do it. To hold out hope for so long. Despite the solitude. Despite years of disappointment. Then to find love. True love. And only have three days. I need to know. How did you convince her in just three days?

SR. COSTA. So strange...the memories that surface when I'm with you. Why is that?

(Remembering.) After I married I used to have this one dream. It came every night at first. Then once a month. Until it seemed to dissolve in my mind like sugar.

MOISES. What was it? Your dream?

SR. COSTA. Water. I remember the river. I was fishing. But I wasn't in a boat. And it was cloudy. But not the sky. The water. I was in the water. Swimming alone. I was an ache as long as this river. So desperately alone. And then I see her. She's on the dock helping her father. She laughs and I feel my whole body tremble. And I know. It's her. She's the one I've been looking for.

And then I'm down on one knee before her. Her hand in mine and she says, "Yes." She says, "Yes."

And just before the sun sets I slip my ring on her finger. And the village priest pronounces us man and wife. Man...and wife.

And then I wake up. I wake up and my beloved is there beside me. Such a wonderful dream. Such a wonderful, wonderful dream.

MOISES. Yes, it is.

(The two men exit with the fish as lights shift to evening.)

Scene Four

*(The evening is filled with the soundscape of
the rainforest and far off the sound of voices.
A party.)*

*(**HELENA** enters, in tears, wearing the nicest
dress she owns. She runs to the end of the
pier. **SRA. COSTA** enters as if following her
daughter.)*

SRA. COSTA. *Filha.*

*(**HELENA** is surprised her mother is here. She
tries very hard to look like she is not crying.)*

HELENA. *Mãe*, I was just... I was just...

SRA. COSTA. Shhh... There's no need. Sit down, Helena.
I want to talk to you.

(They both sit.)

I know this hasn't been an easy time for you. Your
sister's wedding.

HELENA. *(Protesting.) Mãe*, no, it's not –

SRA. COSTA. And I know it isn't Vanity or Pride that haunts
you... It's Duarte.

HELENA. I don't know what you mean.

SRA. COSTA. Helena, you don't have to pretend for me,
filha. You spend so much energy trying not to show
what your heart feels. It's all right. I know.

*(**HELENA** begins to cry. **SRA. COSTA** holds her.
Neither of them see **DUARTE** enter. He remains
hidden, listening and watching.)*

And besides, I have a memory.

You and Duarte. That was the wedding I always
thought I'd see.

When you were children, you thought we couldn't
see you two holding hands. You both tried so hard to
conceal it.

And then everything changed from one day to the next. There was your little sister wedged between you two.

It wasn't easy, *filha*. I felt so helpless. Sometimes I wondered if I should have intervened.

I love you both. But I won't lie that it's Belmira who has worried me. I worried she wouldn't know how to choose a good man. But Duarte is a good and honorable man.

And you, *filha*. I've never worried. I know that when you make your choice it will be the right one.

(**BELMIRA**'s *voice calls from far off.*)

BELMIRA. (*Offstage.*) Duarte. Duarte, *onde você está?*

(**DUARTE** *exits. The women turn towards* **BELMIRA**'s *voice but do not see* **DUARTE** *leave.*)

(**SRA. COSTA** *tenderly wipes the tears from* **HELENA**'s *face.*)

SRA. COSTA. Do something for me, Helena. Spend time with *Senhor* Lira. And I'm not saying it because I'm thinking of his money. I know you can determine his true worth, but only if you at least consider him.

A heart can heal, *filha*. You have loved once. That's a good thing. It means your heart knows how.

You can love again. I promise you.

(*Beat.*)

Did I ever tell you how I met your father?

HELENA. No. Never.

SRA. COSTA. All the women in my village thought I was a lost cause. An old maid. All of twenty-six years old and still unmarried. But your grandfather insisted I not marry unless I could stand before God and family and promise to love a man for the rest of my life. That once I was married my life would be tied to his. My fate. Forever. So I had to choose wisely.

I chose to wait.

I had seen my childhood friends choose poorly. Saw how their lives had become a prison. And I was afraid, too. Afraid I would waver. Would let fear guide my choice instead of my heart. So I prayed for strength.

And then one morning he appeared on the horizon like a new day.

Your father arrived in his boat to trade and sell fish. When our eyes met, it was as if I was looking into myself. And I couldn't look away. He smiled. And I smiled right back. I couldn't help it, as if we were each other's reflection. As if we recognized in one another that part of us that has no words. And I knew.

You'll know, too. I promise.

> *(**SRA. COSTA** kisses **HELENA** and then rises.* *
> **HELENA** *begins to rise as well.)*

No, *filha.* It's all right. You don't have to come back.

> *(**SRA. COSTA** goes to exit stage left. **SR. COSTA*** *
> *enters and finds his wife. He embraces her,* *
> *and they slow dance.)*

SR. COSTA. There you are, *querida.* How am I supposed to dance if my partner has wandered off?

SRA. COSTA. I'm here, *amor.* Here in your arms, now and forever.

> *(They kiss. **HELENA** watches. **SRA. COSTA*** *
> *and **SR. COSTA** dance and then unexpectedly* *
> **SR. COSTA** *carries off **SRA. COSTA** like a* *
> *caveman – she squeals with delight and* *
> *laughter.)*

> *(**HELENA** smiles after them. She takes off her* *
> *shoes and dips her toes into the water.)*

> *(**MOISES** enters stage left. **HELENA** hears him* *
> *and composes herself. **MOISES** sits down next* *
> *to **HELENA**.)*

MOISES. You are alone?

HELENA. I am as you find me.

MOISES. Not at your sister's banquet.

HELENA. Belmira would have us celebrate all month if she could. I think I've had my fill of crowds and noise.

MOISES. I don't think I could ever tire of company. You are so fortunate to be surrounded by family and friends like this.

HELENA. And you? Are you just as...fortunate?

MOISES. No, I am not. I spend a lot of my time alone.

HELENA. That sounds lovely. Here, even when you close your eyes it feels like someone's there behind your eyelids. I would give anything for a sliver of solitude to retreat into.

MOISES. *(Admonishing.)* Don't do that. Don't romanticize solitude. There is nothing lovely about isolation.

(A slightly awkward beat.)

Helena, do you know what it means to feel lonely?

HELENA. I think so. I've always lived inside my head. I'm not afraid to be alone.

MOISES. That's only because you've never been truly alone. Never gone months without...contact.

HELENA. But being near people doesn't mean you feel connected to them. The truth is I've lived almost my entire life alone, surrounded by people but somehow set apart. I've never truly found anyone who could match me thought for thought.

MOISES. All I have are my thoughts. An ocean of them. And I've been adrift for so long, Helena. Searching for someone who could navigate them with me.

HELENA. Someone whose heart can become a map...

MOISES. ...leading us home.

(They become caught in a glance.)

HELENA. When Belmira and I were children, we used to play a staring game.

MOISES. How do you play it?

HELENA. You stare into each other's eyes and the first one to blink loses.

(They begin a staring game. The longer they play, the more they smile. **MOISES** *loses and they laugh.)*

MOISES. We'll have to play again.

HELENA. What? Do you have trouble with losing?

MOISES. Not at all.

(They begin another staring game.)

Tell me, Helena. What do you see, in my eyes?

HELENA. You have a good heart.

And you? What do you see in mine?

MOISES. I see myself. Reflected in the dark pools of your eyes. I could fall right in. Dive to their very depths.

*(***HELENA*** *smiles to herself, turns away bashful.)*

(Playful.) What? What are you thinking?

HELENA. So many nights I've come out to this pier. Dipped my toes in this river and listened to the night come alive with sound. But tonight. Tonight there is something in the air. Something magical.

And you. Your words. What a spell you weave. Like nothing I've ever heard before.

MOISES. Don't fall in love with my words, Helena. Anyone can learn to gather them up like flowers and lay them at your feet.

HELENA. And, what do you lay down?

MOISES. Myself.

(Beat.)

Tell me, Helena. Have you ever been in love?

HELENA. ...Yes.

MOISES. ...What happened?

HELENA. He...

Loving someone isn't always enough. Before they can love you, they have to see you, the real you that lies beneath the surface and he...he loves another.

MOISES. Do you regret loving him?

HELENA. ...No.

I was fourteen. It was a night like this. Balmy and full of promise.

He said my mouth was like a flower. Soft and fragrant. He plucked an orchid from a tree. Tucked it into the folds of my hair. I was his flower, he said. And his alone. I didn't say anything. Just let him kiss me. His mouth was salty and my heart raced. I was afraid my father would catch us. I told him, I would wear this flower for him and only him.

(Pained.) The day I saw him with Belmira on his arm, he wouldn't even look at me. But I kept wearing the flower. A beacon in plain sight calling out to him. A beacon that became a memorial. I buried my heart, placed a flower on its altar and tried to forget.

But how could I when every day I was reminded, when...

> (**HELENA** *turns away from* **MOISES** *to hide her tears.*)

I'm sorry, I – I need a moment to myself.

MOISES. Of course.

But Helena, I hope one day you'll let me be the man who takes up the burden of your tears.

> (**MOISES** *walks to exit stage left. He passes* **DUARTE** *who enters. The men pause to acknowledge one another.* **MOISES** *exits and Duarte approaches* **HELENA**.)

DUARTE. Helena.

HELENA. Duarte.

> (**HELENA** *quickly wipes her eyes.*)

DUARTE. You left early.

HELENA. Yes. I needed some time to myself.

What are you doing here? That dinner is for you and Belmira.

DUARTE. ...I need to speak with you.

HELENA. What about?

DUARTE. *(Apologetic.)* I... I feel the need to explain myself.

HELENA. What is there to explain?

DUARTE. ...I heard you and your mother talking.

HELENA. That was a private conversation.

DUARTE. One that concerns me.

HELENA. Whatever there is to say is in the past. And tomorrow you will be my sister's husband. That is all we should concern ourselves with.

> (**HELENA** *tries to walk past* **DUARTE** *to exit. He takes her hand. She freezes in her tracks at his touch.*)

DUARTE. Do you remember when we were children? How we played together?
Helena?

HELENA. ...My mother called you my shadow.

DUARTE. Almost as if you couldn't tell where one stopped and the other began.
Everything changed so quickly. One day you and I were running through the trees playing. The next your sister was on my arm. Asking me to be her guide. To protect her.
Our village, it turns out, is made up of eyes. People started talking. And then my father sat me down. He told me that to be an honorable man means recognizing one's duty. To do what is expected of you.
For family.
For the village.

> (*Neither* **HELENA** *nor* **DUARTE** *see* **BELMIRA** *enter. She remains on the periphery.*)

...But it was the wrong sister I found myself tied to.

> (*A moment as* **BELMIRA** *takes this in – something inside her breaks.*)

I want you to know that I will be a good husband. I won't abandon her. I won't mistreat her.

But I will not love her. Not the way a husband should. She will always be a little sister to me.

HELENA. Why are you telling me this?

DUARTE. Because I love you.

> (**BELMIRA** *exits.*)

I needed to say that. Even if I only get to say it once. I'll have enough regrets in this life. But not telling you. That is one I cannot live with.

HELENA. But you can live with marrying a woman you do not love...are you a coward?

DUARTE. *(Resigned.)* I must be.

Give me a net. Give me hard labor. Give me sweat and a fish on the other end of the line to fight with. These things make sense to me. These things I can put my hands on and tame.

But what rises in my chest at night. Those wordless thoughts that enter at the back of my mind...they have no form. No texture. I... I don't know how to reel them in, how to tame them.

HELENA. Did you try?

DUARTE. Helena, please. It was like being unable to wake from a dream. Everything was set into motion before I realized the shape it was taking.

I hesitated.

And I thought you... I thought you would protest.

HELENA. Me? Why didn't you protest?

DUARTE. Because I couldn't put words to it. There was just a feeling...an unease that felt...predestined.

HELENA. So you became resigned to your fate.

DUARTE. ...Yes.

HELENA. Why?

DUARTE. ...Because you were right. I'm a coward.

> (**DUARTE** *takes* **HELENA**'s *hand and kisses it.*)

Forgive me.

> (**DUARTE** *exits.* **HELENA** *watches him go and turns away from the sight of him. Something inside her breaks and she tries to suppress the oncoming heartache.* **HELENA** *walks back to the edge of the pier and eventually as the night comes to an end she plucks the flower from her hair, looks at it, closes her hand around the flower, crushing it, and then lets the flower fall from her hand into the river. She is free. Lights shift.*)

Scene Five

(Catharsis, a slow transition to dawn. The sun rises on **HELENA** *still standing at the end of the pier as if she's been there the entire night.* **MOISES** *enters.)*

MOISES. *(Somewhat urgent.)* Helena.

*(***HELENA*** turns, sees that it is* **MOISES**. *She moves towards him. He moves towards her.)*

(They embrace. They kiss.)

It is a new day, *querida.*

HELENA. No. You are the "new day." Fished from the river, from my father's own nets. Welcomed in my home. And now...welcome in my heart.

MOISES. Do you mean that?

HELENA. Yes.

MOISES. Because I don't want you to choose me just because you couldn't be with Duarte, because you're afraid of being alone. I want you to choose me for the same reason I choose you...because I love you.
Helena, I need to know right now Do you love me? Do you really love me?

HELENA. Yes. I do. I do. I didn't think it was possible. To fall in love like this, to really love someone in so short a time. But there is no reason, no words for it. But I know it. When I look into your face and see myself reflected back at me. I feel it, deep inside.

MOISES. ...And Duarte? Do you still feel something for him?

HELENA. ...Yes. But it's different now. Something's changed. Something in me. I'm not the same person I was three days ago. How is that possible?

MOISES. Love. It can transform a person. Genuine love, true love, can break any bond this world places on us.

HELENA. Do you really think that's true?

MOISES. I know it is. Where I come from my people believe that if a woman truly gives you her heart, her love...she frees you.

HELENA. Frees you from what?

MOISES. From a solitude as deep and wide as the Amazon, as cold and dark as its murky waters.

HELENA. Solitude is easy enough to break, my love.

MOISES. Not mine. I need a special kind of woman to love me. I need you.

HELENA. I am yours. My heart. My life. My fate. I tie myself to you.

> *(They kiss.)*

MOISES. I have something for you.

> *(On bended knee **MOISES** takes a ring box from his coat pocket. He opens the ring box and presents the ring.)*

All I've ever asked is that I find you. How long I've searched for you, Helena. Searched year after aching year for the woman that would release me. Whose love would change everything.

Will you wear it?

HELENA. Yes!

> *(**MOISES** slides the ring onto **HELENA**'s ring finger. He closes the ring box and puts it back in his pocket. He takes **HELENA** in his arms and swings her about. They kiss.)*

MOISES. Come, we mustn't waste any time.

HELENA. Where are we going?

MOISES. To find a priest. We have to say our vows in His presence.

> *(**HELENA** stops.)*

HELENA. But... Moises, you don't mean for us to marry today?

MOISES. I do. I intend to marry you before sunset. Right here on this pier. Under this cathedral of trees we'll bind our fates together in the last rays of the setting sun.

HELENA. But...but today is my sister's wedding.

MOISES. A double wedding. All the more cause for celebration.

HELENA. But we can't.

MOISES. Why not?

HELENA. Because...because this day belongs to Belmira and Duarte. We can't trespass on it. My sister would never forgive me, and even I wouldn't blame her.

Besides, why must we hurry?

MOISES. I can't wait.

Helena, please, listen to me. If we don't marry by sunset tonight... I won't be able to return for another year.

HELENA. I don't understand.

MOISES. Do you love me?

HELENA. Yes!

MOISES. Then trust me. Once we marry, nothing will have a hold on me. I'll be free to stay here with you for the rest of our lives. But we must marry today.

HELENA. *Querido*, what aren't you telling me? You ask me to trust you; then you must trust me.

(**MOISES** *walks to the end of the pier.*)

Moises?

MOISES. ...Three days in June. That's all I'm given. Every year I come ashore, every year I am disappointed. I've been searching for so long, Helena. Searching for a woman to see beneath the surface of who I am. To see the part of me that has no words. To recognize in me something of herself. To love me. To really love me and give me her heart truly and freely. Because only then, only then can I stay. Only then will her love transform me, keep me here...as her husband.

And now...to get so close only to be told I must wait. To be cursed with another year of loneliness? I can't bear it, Helena. Because if I remain unmarried on this third day, when the sun dips beneath the Amazon...so must I.

Helena, I need you to make a leap of faith. For me. For us.

(**HELENA** *puts a bit of distance between herself and* **MOISES**.)

HELENA. The old women in the village used to tell us stories when we were girls. A story about three days in June. About men who weren't really men. And they told us, if you meet a man in the month of June, ask him to remove his hat. Run your hand over the flat surface of his forehead so that you know he is a man and not a...
(*Upset.*) It's a story! An old wives' tale. Something to tell little girls.

(**MOISES** *gets on his knees and takes* **HELENA**'s *hands in his.*)

MOISES. Helena, please. Hold on to what you felt for me. To what lies deep inside you. You love me. You love me.

HELENA. ...What are you?

MOISES. I am Moises. Your "new day." Fished from the river from your father's own nets. Welcomed in your home. And...welcomed in your heart.

HELENA. But tell me you are a man.

MOISES. ...Helena, please.

HELENA. Say it.

MOISES. Marry me. Today. And I'll say it tomorrow and every day after.

HELENA. I – I can't. I don't –

(**HELENA** *takes off the ring and puts it in* **MOISES**'s *hand. She begins to back away from him toward stage left.*)

MOISES. Helena!

(**HELENA** *runs and exits stage left leaving* **MOISES** *alone on the pier. Something inside him breaks, and he tries to suppress the oncoming heartache.)*

(Enter **BELMIRA**. *She approaches* **MOISES**.*)*

BELMIRA. Love is for the bold, *Senhor* Lira, and unfortunately my sister is not as bold as she could be.

MOISES. She may yet surprise you.

BELMIRA. No. You forget, I know my sister far better than you do. She's afraid. Of herself...of you.

She's never been good at dealing with the unknown. And what is Love but the unknown? The uncertainty of another. To navigate Love is to fight against the current. And she won't fight for you. It's not in her nature and you know it.

MOISES. I thought...

BELMIRA. What? Did you really think the two of you would sail off into the sunset? Live happily ever after.

MOISES. Yes... I did.

BELMIRA. It's time to grow up, Moises.

Come, let's go for a walk.

(They exit. Two broken hearts. Lights shift.)

Scene Six

(Time passes.)

*(**SRA. COSTA** enters the Costa home, drops off **BELMIRA**'s veil and new wedding dress. **SRA. COSTA** exits.)*

*(**BELMIRA** enters the Costa home. Solemnly she looks at her wedding dress and eventually puts it on.)*

HELENA. *(Offstage.)* Mãe!

*(**HELENA** enters.)*

Have you seen *Mãe*?

BELMIRA. She's been at the church. She's been looking for you. Everyone has.

HELENA. Everyone?

BELMIRA. *Mãe, pai...* Duarte.

HELENA. I need to find *Mãe,* I need to talk to her.

BELMIRA. She'll be here soon.

*(**BELMIRA** presents her back to **HELENA**.)*

Can you help me with this?

*(**HELENA** helps button the back of **BELMIRA**'s dress.)*

Is there anything you want to say to me?

HELENA. *(Flustered.)* Oh – of course. Belmira, you look beautiful.

BELMIRA. You say that as if your heart isn't in it.

HELENA. Belmira, no – of course I mean it. It's just – a lot has happened since I last saw you.

BELMIRA. So I've heard.

HELENA. What does that mean?

BELMIRA. You left the banquet early.

HELENA. Yes. I needed some time alone.

BELMIRA. And did you get it? Time alone, I mean.

HELENA. No I... That's why I need to speak with *Mãe*.

BELMIRA. Yes. You keep saying that.

    Maybe I can help. Maybe you can tell me what's wrong – what's bothering you.

HELENA. No. Thank you, but it doesn't concern you.

BELMIRA. *(Vexed.)* Isn't my sister my concern?

HELENA. That's not what I meant.

BELMIRA. Or, did you mean to say that your little sister isn't grown up enough to understand your problems. Is that it?

HELENA. Of course not. Belmira, what's wrong? Why are you acting like this?

BELMIRA. Like what? Like the child you all think I am? You're only two years older than I am, Helena. I know just as much as you do about the world.

HELENA. I don't think you're a child.

BELMIRA. Then why won't you confide in me? What's so important – so secretive – that you can only tell *Mãe*?

HELENA. I told you. It has nothing to do with you.

BELMIRA. Doesn't it?

HELENA. No, it doesn't! Not everything is about you, Belmira. Even if you want it to be.

BELMIRA. Do you think I wanted this?

    This is your fault, Helena.

HELENA. My fault? What are you talking about, Belmira?

BELMIRA. I'm talking about you. My sister. My only sister. Who knows me better than anyone. Who hides her true feelings. Who's too afraid to go after what she wants. And for that she blames me.

    But you're the one who needs to take responsibility for your silence. For your secrets. Your grudges.

    Do you know the harm you've done?

HELENA. That's you, Belmira. You're the one who causes harm.

BELMIRA. And what have I done?

HELENA. You take everything! Everything that catches your eye, you grab.

BELMIRA. The truth is you despise me. Not because I take what I want in this life, but because I'm not afraid to. And why shouldn't I?

HELENA. Because nothing ever satisfies you. Not this village. Not your life.

BELMIRA. I want to see the world, Helena! Don't blame me that the world we were born into says I have to be a wife to do so. Because if I could, I'd go at it alone. But I can't. So I have to find the best way out.

HELENA. No matter the cost to others? What about loyalty? What about family? You put yourself and your dreams before everything and everyone else.

BELMIRA. Don't talk to me about loyalty, Helena. Don't stand there and pretend you're any better than me. You cause just as much heartache.

HELENA. I'm nothing like you.

BELMIRA. And that's why you'll never be happy.

HELENA. You're right about one thing, Belmira. I do know you. Better than anyone. You're selfish. Impulsive. You don't look before you leap. Don't consider how your actions hurt those around you.

BELMIRA. How I hurt others?

You're the one who runs away from Love. You push people away when they offer you the world. That's why Duarte would rather marry a girl he loves only like a little sister, instead of you.

HELENA. What?

BELMIRA. "I will not love her. Not the way a husband should."

HELENA. Belmira...

BELMIRA. Now, if you'll excuse me, I can't keep my groom waiting.

HELENA. Belmira! Belmira, wait!

(**SRA. COSTA** *enters as* **BELMIRA** *starts to exits.*)

SRA. COSTA. What's going on?

BELMIRA. Helena needs to speak with you, *Mãe.*

>   (**BELMIRA** *exits.*)

SRA. COSTA. Helena, your sister's wedding is in less than an hour and you two are fighting?

HELENA. *Mãe* –

SRA. COSTA. And you're not even dressed yet?

>   (**SRA. COSTA** *begins to help* **HELENA** *undress down to her slip.*)

HELENA. *Mãe*, I need to talk to you.

SRA. COSTA. And where have you been? You were supposed to help me decorate the church –

HELENA. *Senhor* Lira proposed, *Mãe*!

SRA. COSTA. Oh, Helena!

>   (**SRA. COSTA** *embraces* **HELENA** *who continues to cry.*)

Qual é o problema? What is it? What's the matter? Did you say yes?

HELENA. I did. But then I … I don't know what to do.

SRA. COSTA. Because of Duarte?

HELENA. No. It's something else.

SRA. COSTA. What do you feel for *Senhor* Lira? Do you love him?

HELENA. I think I do. That's what scares me.

SRA. COSTA. Oh, *filha,* that's natural. The first time I kissed your father I almost fainted.

HELENA. But *Mãe*, he wants to marry me today.

SRA. COSTA. Today?

HELENA. Yes. In fact, he's insisting on it.

SRA. COSTA. He doesn't waste any time. But some men are like that, Helena. They recognize very quickly the woman they've searched for all their lives.

>   (**SRA. COSTA** *hugs* **HELENA.**)

HELENA. ...*Mãe* do you remember those stories about *botos*?

SRA. COSTA. What stories?

HELENA. About men who aren't really men. River dolphins who come ashore in the month of June.

SRA. COSTA. Oh, Helena! You sound like my mother. I didn't think you believed in superstitions and old wives' tales.

HELENA. Then you remember the stories?

SRA. COSTA. Of course, I do. They almost came between me and your father.

HELENA. What do you mean?

SRA. COSTA. Your father. I met him in the month of June, just like your *Senhor* Lira. My mother, she was a superstitious woman. And she was suspicious of your father because he was a stranger to our village, because he wanted to marry after only three days of courtship.

My entire village thought I was crazy, marrying a man I knew so little about. But your father asked me to listen to my heart, to what it was trying to tell me. And that's what I did, Helena. I listened to my heart. Not to the other people in the village. Not to superstitions or old wives' tales. And *olha* your father and I have been married for twenty years now.

HELENA. *(A realization.)* You only knew *pai* for three days before you married him?

SRA. COSTA. He asked me to take a leap of faith. And I did, *filha*. And each day I loved him more and more. I knew. When I first met him, I knew. This was the man I would spend the rest of my life with. And if you feel that when you look at Moises, then *filha*, marry him. Marry him.

HELENA. I don't understand and I don't completely know, but I feel it. Deep inside. And that part of me that has no words now has one. One word it says over and over again: Moises.

I love him, *Mãe*.

SRA. COSTA. Then God bless you both. And if he insists on marrying you today, don't worry, I'll talk to Belmira and Duarte. We'll do a double wedding.

Of course! You can wear Belmira's first wedding dress. It's fate, *filha.*

(**SRA. COSTA** *takes out* **BELMIRA**'s *first wedding dress and hands it to* **HELENA**.)

Here.

(**SRA. COSTA** *helps* **HELENA** *put on the wedding dress.*)

HELENA. But, *Mãe.* I have to find Moises. I have to tell him. He thinks I...he thinks I don't want him.

SRA. COSTA. Don't worry, *filha.* The moment he sees you dressed as his bride he'll know what's in your heart.

(**SRA. COSTA** *takes a look at her daughter dressed a bride.*)

Oh, Helena. You're going to be very happy, *filha.* I promise.

(*They hug.*)

Come now. Everyone will be heading to the church. Let's go find your groom.

(**SRA. COSTA** *and* **HELENA** *exit.*)

(*Lights shift.*)

Scene Seven

(Transition to dusk. The sunlight is beginning to wane. In the distance the sound of church bells tolling. **MOISES** *walks down to the end of the pier.)*

(After a moment **BELMIRA** *enters. Slowly she walks to the end of the pier and joins* **MOISES** *– they are together yet alone.)*

BELMIRA. When will they arrive?

MOISES. At sunset. Not a moment before.

BELMIRA. And you really haven't seen them in years?

MOISES. Yes. My family...they only gather for weddings. They'll see what is to become of me and then go.

BELMIRA. How nice. I can't wait to meet them. And my family, I don't think they'll be all that surprised at how today has turned out.

MOISES. What do you mean?

BELMIRA. I told you. I overheard Helena and Duarte talking. They have each other now.

MOISES. Then this is what she wants?

BELMIRA. Want has nothing to do with it. Helena isn't motivated by desire. She's motivated by fear. That's why she left you alone on this pier. That's why she told you she loved you and then took it all back.

(Beat.)

MOISES. I thought I had found true love. I thought I wouldn't settle for anything less.

BELMIRA. Life is about navigating disappointments, Moises. And now you have someone who will do that with you.

*(**BELMIRA** approaches **MOISES**, he moves away from her.)*

You told me you didn't want to leave alone. That you wanted someone who would be forever at your side.

I can be that someone. You don't have to be alone ever again.

It's up to you.

MOISES. Nothing turned out the way I thought it would. Maybe the stories I grew up with are just that – stories. And they can only comfort you for so long before...

BELMIRA. Shhhh...you don't need stories anymore. Neither of us do. We can comfort each other now.

>(*Beat.*)

It's almost sunset. Such a romantic start to our new lives.

MOISES. Yes, your life will be very different after today.

BELMIRA. I've always known I wasn't meant to stay in this village. I was meant for something bigger. To see the world.

MOISES. How right you are. And how wrong.

BELMIRA. Are you a riddle now? I love riddles.

MOISES. I don't think you'll love how this one ends.

I hope you can learn to forgive me.

BELMIRA. (*Teasingly.*) Forgive you? What have you done?

MOISES. I lost my faith. In myself. In Love. I can't bear the solitude anymore.

BELMIRA. You won't be alone. You have me.

MOISES. Then I accept you. However imperfect a substitute you are.

BELMIRA. (*Hurt.*) I will help you forget all about my sister. Do not worry. She will become only a memory. Like a dream you can barely recall.

>(**MOISES** *takes a ring from his pocket.*)

MOISES. (*Eventually.*) This ring. It was meant for Helena.

BELMIRA. It'll still fit me.

>(**BELMIRA** *offers her hand.* **MOISES** *looks stage left as if hoping to see* **HELENA**.)

Moises, this is the best decision...for both of us.

MOISES. "Best" does not always mean "right."

BELMIRA. You'd rather leave alone?

> *(A moment of resignation,* **MOISES** *takes* **BELMIRA***'s hand and slips the ring onto her finger.)*

MOISES. With this ring, I bind myself to you. And to the fate that must follow.

> *(***BELMIRA** *kisses* **MOISES***. He doesn't kiss back. Ominous thunder. A storm approaches.)*

BELMIRA. So where are they? You said your family was coming at sunset. Where's your big boat?
I can't wait to see the ocean. How many days do you think it will take us to reach the coast?

> *(The sound of splashing in the water, dolphin clicks.)*

MOISES. I didn't say they were coming in a boat.

> *(Voices from off stage. Lightning, pink, flashes as the storm gets closers.)*

DUARTE, HELENA, SRA. COSTA & SR. COSTA. *(Offstage.)* Belmira! Belmira!

> *(***MOISES** *wraps his arm around* **BELMIRA***'s waist.* **BELMIRA** *reads* **MOISES***'s face and realizes something is amiss. The sun begins to set.* **DUARTE, SRA. COSTA, SR. COSTA,** *and* **HELENA** *enter from stage left.)*

HELENA. Moises!

> *(***MOISES** *sees* **HELENA** *and painfully realizes that she is wearing a wedding dress.)*

MOISES. *(To* **HELENA.***)* Forgive me!

> *(***MOISES** *picks up* **BELMIRA** *as if carrying his bride over the threshold. He leaps off the pier into the Amazon River, taking* **BELMIRA** *with him.* **BELMIRA** *screams.)*

(**SRA. COSTA** *collapses in her husband's arms.*
HELENA *and* **DUARTE** *run to the end of the pier.*
DUARTE *has to hold* **HELENA** *back, his arm*
around her waist as she tries to throw herself
into the river after **MOISES**.*)*

HELENA. *(Inconsolable.)* Moises! Moises!

(*It begins to rain. A deluge. Pink lightning*
strikes, and the lights go completely dark.
The thunder rumbles and slowly dissipates.
Lights shift.)

Epilogue

(Sunset. A year later. **HELENA** *sits on the edge of the pier, a basket in her lap. Intermittently she throws fish into the water. The sound of the bait hitting water.)*

HELENA. My father spent weeks searching the river for the both of you.

Nothing.

No sign. No trace.

You're like a secret the river won't give up.

This river. It seems...quieter. Before I used to see a *boto* at least once a week. Now...*nada.*

When I walk through our village I can hear the old women whispering. It should have been me, they say.

But they don't know. Don't know that if it had been me, I would have kept you here. My love...it would have transformed you.

Since that day. Since you left. Nothing in this life has felt real. I have to touch things to know they're really there.

Even me.

As if I'm just a reflection. A trick of light.

(Beat.)

Maybe I didn't deserve happiness. I hesitated. You asked me to take a leap of faith and I flinched. I left you here alone on this pier.

It happened so quickly, our three days. So quickly.

And I began to second-guess myself. Our love. That you even existed. But then there's my sister. Her absence is the only proof you were real. And the hole she created in our lives, Duarte crawled right through it. Right through it to me.

There he was. Every day for three months. Trying to extinguish any smoldering thought of you with his presence. He tried, in his own way, to tell me that this is how things were meant to end.

I don't really believe that.

But he wore me down, Moises. Eroded so much I felt myself disappearing.

How I wouldn't deserve you now.

*(**DUARTE** enters and approaches her.)*

DUARTE. Helena. Come inside, *querida*. You'll wear yourself out.

HELENA. I'm fine. Really.

DUARTE. Then come in for your mother's sake. She doesn't like you coming to the pier.

HELENA. Imagine that. A fisherman's wife afraid of the water.

(Beat.)

It's been a year. To the very day.

DUARTE. ...I know.

Helena, please. Your mother needs you.

HELENA. My mother. She's convinced the whole village. Even herself. But Belmira didn't drown. I know what I saw. You saw it, too. How her dress. When it got wet. How it transformed in the water. How they both changed –

DUARTE. *(Interrupting.)* I don't know what I saw. None of us do. The water was too murky.

> *(**HELENA** suffers to hear his denial. **DUARTE** puts his hand on her shoulder. She removes his hand from her shoulder and holds it in both of hers.)*

HELENA. In a moment. I promise. Just give me a few more minutes.

Alone.

> *(**DUARTE** leaves. **HELENA** watches him leave. After he's gone she stands up on her own revealing her pregnant belly. **HELENA** takes*

out her pearl necklace that's been hidden beneath her dress collar. As she speaks she takes it off.)

(To the river.) I would have waited for you. Why wouldn't you wait for me? But now...we've all made our choices. For better or worse.

I will be a good wife. I won't abandon him. I won't mistreat him. But... I will not love him. Not as I should. Not as I would have. Had it been you.

Forgive me.

(HELENA throws her necklace into the river. We hear it splash. As lights fade we hear more splashing, something in the water. In the dark, dolphin clicks echo.)

End of Play

Printed in the USA
CPSIA information can be obtained
at www.ICGtesting.com
CBHW082000240324
5781CB00029BA/617

9 780573 70896